BILL WALLACE

Goosed!

Drawings by Jacqueline Rogers

Aladdin Paperbacks
New York London Toronto Sydney

To Carrol and Jack Pruitt and to Terri and Jill —B. W.
For Grace and Emma, with thanks —J. R.

First Aladdin Paperbacks edition May 2004

Text copyright © 2002 by Bill Wallace
Illustrations copyright © 2002 by Jacqueline Rogers
Published by arrangement with Holiday House

ALADDIN PAPERBACKS
An imprint of Simon & Schuster Children's Publishing Division
1230 Avenue of the Americas, New York, NY 10020

The text of this book was set in Versailles Roman.

Manufactured in the United States of America
20 19

The Library of Congress has cataloged the hardcover edition as follows:
Wallace, Bill, 1947-
Goosed! / by Bill Wallace.
p. cm.
Summary: When Jeff's girlfriend leaves a Labrador retriever puppy with his family for a week, his dog T.P. and cat Cord hope the energetic puppy does not stay any longer.
ISBN 0-8234-1757-3(hardcover)
1. Dogs—Juvenile fiction. [Dogs—Fiction. 2. Bird dogs—Fiction. 3. Labrador retriever—Fiction. 4. Cats—Fiction. 5. Pets—Fiction.] I. Title.
PZ10.3.W 162 GO 2002
[Fic]—dc21 2002017112

ISBN-13: 978-0-689-86681-4   ISBN-10: 0-689-86681-X (pbk.)

Chapter 1

It was before daylight when I sensed something. I didn't know what it was.

Normally I stayed in bed until Mama and Daddy were ready to get up. It felt good—safe and cozy—to nestle between them. Mama was especially nice to snuggle with. She didn't flop around as much as Daddy. I could stay there all day if they'd let me.

But this morning felt different. I couldn't get back to sleep, so I decided to go investigate.

When very young, I learned that jumping up and stepping on Daddy's tummy was *not* the way to get out of bed. Barking was even worse. If I barked when someone came to the door, then they'd get up to see who was there. Afterward they'd pat me on the head and tell me what a good boy I was. If there wasn't anybody at the door, well, Daddy would yell at me in his meanest, deepest voice. It would make my ears flatten and my tail tuck. So just to be on the safe side, I had to find out what woke me before coming back to tell them about it.

Flat on my belly, pulling with my elbows and pushing with my hind paws, I crawled to the foot of the bed. Once there I slid quietly over the edge.

Except for the whooshing sound of the heater, the house was silent. Even with the heater blowing, there was a chill in the air. I made my way down the short hall and paused at Jeff's door. All was quiet, so I trotted off to the living room.

I could hear a faint noise from outside the house. A movement. A scratching that didn't belong. There was a smell, too.

Something was there.

The noise and smell came from the front porch. I lay down on my side and tried to

peek under the crack at the bottom of the door. I couldn't see a thing. So after a while I went to the back of the house. The door was closed there, too. But behind the table and chairs where they ate was a bay window. Peeking through the plants that lined the windowsill, I saw it.

Snow.

Just the sight of it made my tail wag. My tail sounded like someone beating on a drum, as it whacked against the flower pot.

I loved snow. I loved to run through it and be the first one to leave tracks in the smooth white. I loved to watch it spray in powdery clouds behind me. I loved the feel of the big flakes on my nose and tongue.

But snow *never* came this late in the year. Quail hunting season was over. Jeff had even talked Daddy and Mama into helping him take the cover off the giant drinking bowl in the backyard.

This was weird. This was exciting. I had to go tell them.

Before I climbed out from under the table, I took one last look at the giant drinking bowl. A little chill raced from my tail to my ears.

Even when the cover was on, I *did not* like the giant drinking bowl. That's because one time I tried to get some water from it and ended up toppling over and falling in. I swam and swam, but there was no way out. If Daddy hadn't swooped me up in the blue net, well . . . From that time on, I stayed well clear of the giant bowl. Cover or not, I didn't want anything to do with that deep water.

A sound perked my ears. It was the noise from the TV. That meant Mama and Daddy were awake. I raced for the bedroom.

Above the noise from the TV, I heard the tall, white drinking bowl flush. That meant Mama was in the bathroom. I wanted to tell her and Daddy about the snow. I flew through the door.

A quick glance was all it took. Daddy was on his side, near the edge of the bed. That meant the rest of the mattress was clear.

One strong leap carried me well above the edge of the bed, over Daddy, and . . .

My eyes flashed!

There was a big lump in our bed. My legs locked, trying to stop myself in midair. Jeff's eyes flashed, as big around as mine probably were. His mouth flew open.

"Uuumphf! T.P.! What in the world . . ."

I hopped to the empty part of the bed.

I'm sorry, I said by tucking my tail and flattening my ears against my head. *I didn't know you were there. You hardly ever crawl in bed with us anymore. I'm sorry.*

"Are you okay, Jeff?" Daddy raised his head from the pillow. "You hurt?"

Jeff moaned again, then stretched out and relaxed.

"I'm okay. Guess T.P. didn't know I was in here. Crazy dog landed right on me."

Instead of trying to swat me, Jeff lay back and reached out a hand. Tail wagging but head still low, I eased up beside him. He petted me a minute and rubbed behind my ears. Then he grabbed me and dragged me across his tummy. With me pinned against him, he rocked back and forth, making a funny growling sound and wrestling me around like we used to do when we were both younger.

"What's going on in here?" Mama yawned.

"Your son came sneaking in to lie down with us. T.P. didn't know he was here and landed smack-dab in his middle."

Mama stood at the edge of the bed until Jeff and I were through wrestling. Jeff scooted over beside Daddy so there would be room for her.

"What are you doing up this early?" she asked Jeff, flipping the sheet back and nestling down beside me. "You always sleep late on Saturday. Forget what day it was?"

"No. Just felt like getting up early."

The whole side of his body tensed where he was holding me. Even his voice was tight and nervous.

Something was wrong.

When he loosened his hold on me, I stood up and leaned forward, sniffing near his mouth.

People are weird animals. They use mouth noises to communicate. But they don't always say what they really mean.

With the rest of us animals, it's different. We use all of our senses to communicate. Not just our ears to listen, but our eyes to watch. We feel things, too. And with me, a bird dog, my sense of smell is especially keen.

Jeff *said* he just felt like getting up early. From sniffing and watching, I could tell what he really *meant* was: "I'm nervous and I couldn't sleep. I'm scared you won't let me keep it."

I sure wondered what "it" was.

Mama cleared her throat. "Just felt like getting up early. Yeah, right. What's going on?"

Guess Mama had a better nose than I thought. She could tell he was lying, too.

Chapter 2

Jeff scooted up in bed and propped my pillow behind his back. "Okay," he began. "It's not any big deal, but . . ."

That's what the mouth noises said. A quick sniff told me that what he really meant was: "Man, this is rough. I'm afraid they're gonna be mad. I sure wish I had some help."

Careful not to step on anyone, I stood up, left my spot between Mama and Jeff, and climbed off the foot of the bed. If Jeff needed help, it was up to me.

"You know Mandy Bowen, right? Her mom and dad raise registered chocolate Labs, right?"

Mama and Daddy didn't say anything.

Standing on my hind feet, I put my paws on the windowsill. Nobody noticed.

"Their female, Lady Elizabeth of Throckmorton, or something like that—I never could remember for sure—anyway, she had this litter of six pups about eight weeks ago."

I nudged the blinds with my nose. "Come look at the snow," I whined.

I had a really good whine. Not loud, but high pitched. That's how I told them I was hungry or needed water. Maybe seeing the snow would keep them from being mad at Jeff.

"And she really had problems, I guess. She can't have any more pups. And anyway . . . ah . . . well . . ."

He was really having trouble now. He was stammering: getting the mouth noises all tangled up inside his head before they could come out. I whined louder and got my nose between two of the plastic louvers. If I lifted them, maybe they could see the white.

Daddy rolled over so he could look at

Jeff. "Spit it out, son," he said. "What are you trying to tell us?"

"Okay." Jeff slid down in the bed and kind of tucked the sheet up under his chin. I shook the window blind again.

"Come look at the snow," I barked.

Jeff cleared his throat. "They've sold four of the pups—over five hundred dollars each. They're keeping one of the females. That leaves one pup. And . . . and . . ."

I barked louder. They ignored me.

"And?" Mama urged.

"And they're boarding Lady and the female pup with the vet. And . . . ah . . ."

"And?" Mama urged again.

"And Mandy wanted me to have one of the pups. *For free!* I told her I'd have to ask you and Dad first. But they're leaving for spring break this morning. Going to Memphis to visit Mandy's aunt. So I told her to go ahead and bring the puppy out, when they leave town. I figured, whether you let me keep it or not, the least we could do was baby-sit until they get back next week."

With that, he yanked the sheet up to cover his head, and lay perfectly still.

I pawed the windowsill, bumped the blinds with my nose, and barked.

"T.P.!" Daddy yelled. "What in the world's wrong with you?"

"Quit that!" Mama shouted. "You're scratching the wood."

They both scolded me but neither came to look. They just glared down at the lump in our bed where Jeff hid under the sheets.

I barked again.

Mama swung her feet over the side of the bed and stomped to the window. The blinds clicked when they went up. Light flooded the room.

"My gosh!" she gasped. "It's snow! Come and look at this."

"No way." Dad chuckled. "It never snows this late in the spring."

Jeff shot from under the covers. He patted my head as he rushed by to look out the window.

"Did a good job, didn't I, Jeff?" I wagged my tail. "Got you out of that one."

He didn't even seem to notice.

Daddy didn't hop out of bed like Jeff did. He sat on the edge of the mattress and yawned. Then he scratched his head. Finally he stood up and waddled over to join us. "I can't believe this! I'll bet this sets a new record for the latest snowfall."

Snow fell in big flakes now. Some as round as my paw, they floated from the sky. With no wind to push them, they wove gently back and forth like the easy swaying of Mama's rocking chair. There were so many of them, we could barely see the chain-link fence.

Jeff patted my head again.

"Come on, T.P. Let's go play in the snow."

I bounded off for his room, with Jeff hot on my heels. We hadn't even made it to the door when Mama stopped us.

"Hold on a minute, young man."

Jeff stopped. I circled back to him. Mama stood with her arms folded, glaring at her son.

"When are Mandy and her folks supposed to bring this dog out?"

Dog? Dog! What dog? Nobody said anything about a dog. Jeff said a chocolate Lab.

Jeff cleared his throat. "They said they were going to leave pretty early. But this snow might have slowed them down. I don't know exactly what time. I'll get some clothes on and wait for them out front."

Mama's eyes narrowed to tiny slits.

"You used to pull this stuff when you were little."

Jeff tried to look innocent. "What stuff?"

Daddy stepped up beside Mama and put his arm around her shoulder. "Inviting friends out without asking our permission," he answered for her. "Going over to someone's house without telling us first. Dragging that stray cat home."

"Cord is the best cat we ever had," Jeff argued.

"Cord is the *only* cat we ever had," Mama snapped back. "Now you've given your word that you'd take care of a dog. That *does not* mean you're going to keep it. You already have a dog. *I'm* the one who ends up having to feed the animals, empty the cat box, and pick up the poop out of the yard. Your father and I don't appreciate your pulling this stuff on us—not one little bit."

"Right," Daddy agreed. "We thought you'd outgrown things like this."

Jeff's shoulders sagged. He ducked his head and stared at his feet. My tail wrapped under my tummy.

"You're thinking that if we have the puppy around for a week, we'll fall in love with it and let you keep it," Mama said. "It's not going to work this time. You get dressed and watch for Mandy and her parents. Tell them that as soon as they get back from Memphis, they are to come and take the dog home. Do you understand?"

"Yes, ma'am."

"And," Mama added, "if you ever pull something like this again . . ."

"I won't, Mama. I promise."

Head bowed and shoulders slumped so low his hands dangled almost to his knees, Jeff walked to his room.

I followed him. I'd done all I could.

Sometimes boys get in so much trouble, not even their dog and a good snow can get them out of it.

Chapter 3

What *was* a chocolate Lab?

And why did Mama keep talking about a dog?

I didn't have time to think on it or worry. My boy was sad. When Jeff was sad, it made me sad, too.

I'd thought that getting dressed and playing in the snow would make him feel better. Now I wasn't so sure even that was going to help.

Getting in trouble is *not* fun. When I was little, I made a mess on the carpet a couple of times. Daddy yelled at me and rubbed my nose in the wet spot. I didn't like that at all. One time they forgot and left me inside while they went to a movie. I was lonely and there was nothing to do, so

I started chewing on one of the couch pillows. I can still remember how fun it was to growl, shake my head, and watch the white fluffy stuffing fill the air. It was fun UNTIL . . .

Mama and Daddy came home and found the mess.

Jeff didn't like being in trouble, either. He put on his jeans, a sweatshirt, and two pairs of socks. Then we went to the closet in the playroom to find his boots and a coat.

Since early spring had been so warm, Mama had already put the winter things away. Jeff found his coat and dug around in the chest of drawers until he finally located his cap and gloves.

Still he seemed sad and gloomy as he shuffled to the front door.

Maybe I could get him to chase me. Maybe we could play and romp in the snow. Wrestling, playing tag, and flopping around always cheered him up.

Jeff unlocked the front door. When the bolt rattled, I heard another sound. It was that scratching noise again. Only this time it was louder. There was something out there—and it *wasn't* just snow.

Sometimes—not very often—Jeff went outside and forgot me. I always tried to shoot past before he got out. That way the door didn't slam shut in my face.

Only this time, Jeff didn't step out. He jumped back and slammed the storm door.

Something was there. Something scared him.

Maybe it was a wild animal. Maybe a big, ferocious dog. Or maybe . . .

"Mom. Dad," Jeff called. "We've got a problem."

My hair bristled. Legs stiff, I sucked in a deep breath to make myself look bigger.

"Let me at it," I woofed. "I'll protect you."

I meant exactly what I said.

Only . . . really and truly, my insides kind of hoped he *wouldn't* open the door. I didn't know what was there. It must be something horrible.

"What is it, Jeff?" Daddy asked, pressing his nose against the glass so he could see out, too.

Mama scooted beside Daddy. The front door was big, but not big enough for all three of them. When Mama came to look, Jeff got smushed in the corner against the wooden door.

"It's already here." He pointed at the ground.

Mama frowned. "There's a letter taped to it. Go see what it says."

With all the legs in the way, I couldn't see what was going on. Every time I tried to shove my head through, somebody shifted or moved a leg. I had to be quick just to keep from getting stepped on.

Jeff disappeared through the open doorway. In a second, Daddy stepped to the side and held the door wide so he could come back in.

Only Jeff didn't come back in. A cardboard box came in. Well, Jeff was carrying it. But the box was so big, it hid his chest and face.

With a grunt, Jeff set the box on the floor. Something inside clunked. Then it started scratching again. A smell came to my nose. It smelled sort of like a dog—but not. My ears perked.

There was a white piece of paper stuck on the top of the box. Jeff pulled it off. He opened it, pulled another piece of paper from inside, and stared at it.

"'Dear Jeff,'" he began. "'I wanted to see you before we left on our trip. However, Father listened to the Weather Channel last night. They are predicting snow, moving in from the west. I know this won't happen, as it never snows this time of year. Still he got us up and around at four-thirty so we could beat the storm.

"'He wouldn't even let me call, as he thought it was rude to wake you and your parents so early on a weekend morning.

"'Please take good care of the puppy. She is my favorite of the whole litter. The blanket she sleeps on is in the box, as is her ball. She is quite attached to the ball. Mother says it is probably because we weaned her a bit early.

"'I hope you love her.

"'Love and kisses, Mandy.'"

Jeff kind of mumbled the last part of what he was reading. When he folded the white paper and held it behind his back, his face turned red. Mama's eyebrows arched. Daddy stared at him over the top of his glasses.

"Okay." Jeff shrugged. "She writes mushy letters. It's not my fault."

The box thumped. Then it rocked back and forth. I jumped back. Jeff stuffed the paper in his pocket and leaned over to open it.

"Yap, yap," the box said.

My eyes flashed. My tail stopped wagging in mid-swing.

"Arff, arff."

A chill started at the very tip of my tail. It raced up my back, between my shoulder blades, and stopped at my neck, right behind my ears. It made them stand out and quiver.

The instant Jeff opened the box, "It" sprang out, raced straight for Mama, and bounced against her leg. Then it bounded to Jeff.

This was far worse than some wild animal. This was far more terrifying. This was a . . . a . . .

I didn't know what it was. But it was horrible!

The thing was totally wild. It was all over the place—wiggling, yapping, hopping against Mama's, then Daddy's, then Jeff's legs.

It leaked, too.

Chapter 4

Jeff grabbed for it. He missed. Then the thing spotted me. Eyes wide, and with this gosh-awful, sloppy grin on its face, it charged.

My legs locked. The hair bristled down my back. My lip curled.

"Leave me alone!" I snarled. "I'll tear you apart. I'll eat you alive. I'll . . ."

I never got to finish my threats. The thing broadsided me. Just flew into me like I wasn't even there. I snapped, but I didn't bite. I did knock it off me with my snout. Dirt brown fur, legs, and a tail went tumbling across the carpet.

Four legs. Tail. Fur. Floppy ears. It had to be a dog. It looked like a dog, just smaller. Only it didn't smell like a dog. It had a funny odor that made my nose crinkle. And . . .

When I knocked it away, it leaked again.

The thing scrambled to its feet, shook itself, and charged at me a second time.

"I'll bite you, for sure," I snarled. "I was nice the first time. But if you jump on me again . . ."

It just ran faster.

At the last instant, Jeff's hands darted out and swooped it up. He held the thing at arm's length, so when it leaked he wouldn't get wet, and turned toward the front door.

"I think she's a little excited," he said, with a sheepish grin on his face. "I'll stay on the porch with her for a minute. I'll clean up the dribble spots, too, okay?"

Mama just looked at him. Daddy stared over the top of his glasses and shook his head.

Lip still curled, I didn't move. I was afraid Jeff might open the door and let the thing back inside.

Then I sneezed. And sneezed. And sneezed, and sneezed again.

"T.P., knock it off!" Daddy demanded after the sixth or seventh one.

I forced the snarl from my face and snorted a couple of times. I still got in two more sneezes before I was done.

I just hated it when that happened.

It's hard to look mean and scary when you're sneezing your fool head off. I couldn't help it, though. Long as I could remember, every time I tried to act like a tough guy, I sneezed. When I bared my teeth, I had to curl my lip way up. When I curled my lip way up, the little hairs inside my nose tickled. When my nose tickled, I sneezed. When I sneezed, I just couldn't stop.

Cord, the cat, used to play chase with me. A few times, when we wrestled, he'd get too rough or accidentally jab me with one of his sharp claws. I'd snarl, warning him to take it easy.

We didn't play much anymore, now that I was so much bigger than he was, and Cord was so old. But back when I was a puppy . . .

Puppy?

Puppy! That's what that thing was!

I rushed to the front door. My nose smushed against the glass. For a second I thought the sneezing was going to start all over again. Fighting it off, I looked past the nose print I left and out into the snow-covered yard.

The thing raced in small circles around Jeff. It jumped against his leg, then ran some more. Once it tripped over its big feet and plowed, nose first, through the snow. Big ears flopped when it shook itself off and hopped up.

My perked ears began to droop. They sagged lower and lower until they dangled below my jowls. My tail sank slowly until the tip touched the ground.

It *was* a puppy.

The puppy was playing with *my* Jeff. It was playing in *my* yard and messing up *my* snow.

I whined.

Mama and Daddy ignored me. At this rate, all my snow would be crunched, jumbled, and messed up before I ever got outside.

I whined again.

They didn't even glance down.

Nose practically dragging the carpet on one end, and tail hanging low on the other, I crept to the bedroom. I didn't hop on the bed. I climbed up, tucked myself into a ball, and wrapped my tail over my ear.

Before long they would notice I was gone. They would come to find me. When they saw how sad I was, Daddy would pet me. Mama would rub behind my ears and say sweet things to me. Jeff would maul me around, try to get me to wrestle with him, and make me play. Once they saw how miserable I was, things would be better.

Okay. That didn't work.

It felt like I lay there forever. No one showed up. Maybe if I stayed longer . . .

Staying longer wasn't a choice. First thing in the morning, I really need to go outside. Jumping off the bed, I bounded down the hall and raced to the front door. Through the glass, I saw Jeff sitting in the lawn chair on the porch. The puppy was no place in sight.

I whined.

Nothing happened.

Desperate now, I stood on my hind legs and put my paws on the storm door. Still nothing. So I shoved a couple of times, rattling the glass.

Jeff turned to see what was going on. When he twisted in the chair a bit, I saw the puppy. It was on his *lap*.

Feeling as if someone had kicked me in the tummy, I sat down. Slowly my tail began to tuck. It wrapped tighter and tighter around my rump until I was sitting on it. Then I remembered how much I needed to go.

"This is serious, people," I whined as loud as I could. "I need out!"

When my front paws hit the glass a second time, Jeff wheeled around in the chair and glared at me. I smiled and wagged my tail. He twisted farther and reached for the handle.

The door opened just wide enough for me to get my head out. Then I wiggled my neck and shoulders. When they cleared, I shot through and didn't even slow down to enjoy the feel of the snow under my paws. When I got to the sweet gum tree, I didn't even stop to sniff. I didn't care if some coyote or stray dog had marked over my scent. I just heisted my leg and let 'er rip.

Man, you talk about relief.

"T.P., don't you want to come see the puppy?"

Jeff had ignored me all morning. So I ignored him. Besides, this felt *soooo* good.

"Come on, T.P. Come say hi to the new puppy."

When I finished my business, I didn't so much as look back at him.

"She's really cute," Jeff called from behind me. "I know you're gonna like her."

The air was sharp and cold. The falling snow felt good on my nose. Finally I found a place where it was still crisp and white and not messed up. I licked it, then raced farther. I stopped and marked the big oak tree next to the pasture fence.

First thing in the morning, there were always new and exciting smells from the night. I wanted to sniff along the fence line, then crawl under the barbed wire and go check out the pasture. Instead, I turned back to be with Jeff.

When I got to the porch, he wasn't there. The front door was closed. Standing on my hind legs and barking, I bumped the glass with my front paws to tell him I was ready to come in.

The door didn't open.

I sat down on the porch. Whined.

My boy had forgotten me.

Chapter 5

Forgotten.

Deserted.

Locked out.

What was a faithful, trusting, loving bird dog to do?

I went back to the sweet gum and heisted my leg again.

I'll show him, I thought, kicking snow with my hind feet. When he does remember me, I won't be here. I'll be gone.

Beyond the front yard, where the barbed-wire fence stretched out at the edge of the pasture, there were always smells. The night creatures used the fence line as a pathway. The short grass made it easier to travel. At the slightest noise or movement from houses, the night creatures shot from the yard and into the tall grass on the other side, until the danger passed.

At a slow trot, I followed the fence line to my right. There were smells, but they were all old—some left from two nights ago. When I got to the corner post, I turned and trotted down the hill.

A mouse. Stopping, I lowered my nose to the ground. Ears perked, listening for the slightest noise, I sniffed. A mouse had been there, all right. But it was a good four hours ago. That must have been when snow chased the cold air across here. Now the mouse was buried beneath the snow, all warm and cozy in his pile of grass. I moved on.

Well short of the magic gate, I stopped. It was a strange piece of iron and metal that stretched across the road to our house. We had other gates. There were two in the backyard. Another kept Dandy in her pen. But none of those gates was magic. People opened and closed them. Jeff, Mama, Daddy—someone was always around. They fiddled with something, made a clanking noise, and the gate opened. Once we were outside, they made another clanking noise and the gate closed.

The magic gate . . . well, it opened and closed all by itself. There was no warning. Just a little growl, then it did its thing.

The magic gate seemed to know when Daddy needed to drive his car to work. It opened before he started down the road. It seemed to know when Mama was coming home from grocery shopping. It opened before she got there. Sometimes it opened for no reason at all. But we usually had company not too long afterward. And it knew when they left, too, because it closed when they were gone.

Like I said, I stayed well clear of the magic gate.

The plum patch not far from the corner was always a good place to check for quail. I cut across the pasture to sniff around there.

Nothing. So I headed toward the stand of cedar trees, near the center of the front pasture. I was almost to the cedars when the snow exploded. White powder shot into the air. Just inches from my paw, something burst from a pile of snow and darted down the hill. Long ears. Fuzzy tail.

Rabbit!

I hesitated.

Bird dogs are *not* supposed to chase rabbits. We're supposed to find birds. But rabbits are fun and exciting and they run from you. If no people were around to watch . . .

Crouched low, ears flat against my head, I chased after him. We raced between two big cedars, turned left, and charged over the hill and toward the dry creek bed. I almost got him, once. My legs were longer. Faster. But at the last second, he dodged.

My powerful long legs gained on him again. That fuzzy tail was just inches from my snout when he dropped over the edge of the dry creek bed and darted to the right.

I didn't.

Going straight, I slid down the bank, almost fell, then got myself turned so I could go for him again.

A high, shrill whistle cut the crisp morning air. Jeff stood on the front porch. He whistled again.

"Forget you," I said with a snort. Then I turned my attention back to the rabbit.

He was *way* ahead of me now. I barely got a glimpse of his fuzzy white tail, down where the dry creek bed widened out. Still running at full speed, he darted up the far bank. If I cut across, got the angle on him, I could make up the distance I'd lost when Jeff's whistling made me stop.

Leaping the deep part of the channel, I charged up the steep bank. Once over the ridge, I judged the angle I had to take to cut him off, and . . .

Stopped dead in my tracks.

A huge animal stood not more than ten feet away from me. It didn't move a muscle, just stared at me. Brown fur on its back and lighter fur on its underside. I'd seen an animal like it before, but I just couldn't remember. There was a wild smell—much stronger than the rabbit. In the blink of an eye, it spun and raced up the hill toward the thick stand of elm and hackberry trees.

It ran away from me! Big as the thing was, it was scared of *me*.

Long ears. Fuzzy white tail that stuck straight up in the air. It was longer than the rabbit's tail, but just as white and fuzzy.

A giant rabbit!

I knew it looked familiar. I'd chased one before, but it had been a long time ago.

This thing was enormous. But if it ran . . .

I took off. Snow flew. I ran as fast as I could, but didn't gain on it at all. On the far side of the hill, it disappeared into the trees. I caught a glimpse of it again, near the pond. It slowed. Now was my chance.

Jeff whistled again. I ignored him. Ran as hard as I could.

Just inside the trees, I stopped. I couldn't see it anymore. Sniffing the ground, I found which way it had gone. Before I had taken so much as one single step to follow it, another smell grabbed my nose.

"Wanna go after the deer, Clyde?"

"Nah. Don't reckon so, John," a second voice drawled. "Deer's too fast. Let's eat the dog, instead."

Two scraggly coyotes stood watching me, at the edge of the pond. My legs locked.

My hair bristled. Before I could turn and run, I saw a third one, following from the direction I'd just come.

I was so scared I didn't even sneeze.

I stretched myself as tall as I could, filled my lungs with air, did everything I could to look *BIG*.

It's common knowledge among dogs that coyotes aren't the smartest animals around. They don't even have the good sense to make friends with people. They don't wag their tails so they can get fed. They don't bark and protect the house so they can sleep in a warm doghouse during the winter. They just slink around in the shadows and eat whatever is handy.

Right now *I* was handy.

It's also common knowledge that no matter how big or mean a dog *thinks* he is, on any given day, one coyote can whip three or four dogs.

These guys were hungry. There were three of them. Only one of me.

Taking a deep breath, I growled deep in my throat. "You'd better back off. I'm

tough. I'm mean. You come any closer and I'll tear you apart."

The coyotes just grinned and licked their chops.

I was in trouble. Major trouble.

Chapter 6

The tough guy routine wasn't working. Maybe I should try a different approach.

Forcing the snarl from my face, I tried to wag my tail. It didn't wag. I was so scared, everything was stiff as a frozen field mouse. Mustering all my concentration, I finally forced my tail to swing back and forth.

"Look, fellas. I don't want to fight. I'm a friendly dog. I don't want any trouble."

They just grinned.

"Rump roast looks good to me, John. How about you?"

"Think I'll gnaw me off a hunk of that there shoulder, Clyde. Might be a little stringy, but I'll give 'er a try."

Eyes wide and ears arched so much it looked like I was smiling, I sort of shifted back and forth from one front foot to the other.

"Oh, you guys are hungry, right?"

"We're starved," the one named John growled.

I wagged my tail harder.

"I'm hungry, too. Tell you what. Why don't I help you chase down that giant rabbit. Bet all four of us could catch him. He'd probably taste a lot better than me. You know—not as stringy or tough." The coyote behind me was getting closer. "And . . . and . . . ah, just to prove to you how much I want to be friends, I'll . . . ah . . . I'll let you eat my share. I won't even take a bite. Honest."

"Giant rabbit?"

"Yeah, Clyde." John sneered. "He's so dumb, he thinks the deer was a big rabbit. Can you believe that?"

Both coyotes grinned—but they didn't laugh. Their eyes were on me. They didn't blink. Clyde stayed where he was as John moved to my left. From the corner of my eye, I could barely see the third coyote. She had stopped. But as John moved to my left, she took a couple of steps to my right.

I knew not to let them get behind me. I took a step back. Crouching low to the ground, John moved farther.

Clyde closed in from the front. John was behind me on the left. The third coyote was behind me on the right.

Any second now, they'd charge.

The sharp ridge of fur made my back tingle. I humped my shoulders forward and drew my neck in, protecting my throat. Sucking as much air as I could hold, I barked.

The bark was so loud and ferocious, it startled me. I'd never made a sound like that before. I could hardly believe it.

Suddenly Clyde's eyes flashed. His ears perked so high they looked like tiny, sharp mountain peaks on his head. He spun and raced into the darkness of the trees. Tails tucked, John and the third coyote were hot on his heels.

That surprised me even more than my

bark had. I couldn't believe I'd scared them off.

"And don't come back," I woofed. Taking a couple of steps, I pretended to chase them. "If I ever catch you on our property again, I'll tear you to shreds. I'll rip you apart. I'll—"

"T.P.! Get up here."

The sudden voice from behind made me jump.

Jeff stood on the crest of a little hill. Fists on his hips and eyes narrow, he frowned at me.

"Did you see 'em?" I woofed. "There were *three* of them. Coyotes. They were—"

"I saw that deer go flying across the pasture," Jeff interrupted. "You know you're not supposed to chase deer and rabbit. I whistled for you ten minutes ago! Where have you been? You get your tail up here—right now!"

I glanced back to where the coyotes had vanished into the forest. Then I looked at Jeff.

Okay, my ferocious bark was impressive. But that wasn't what scared the coyotes away. Here I was, feeling all brave and powerful and scary. It was a little depressing to find out that I'd had help.

On the other hand—if it hadn't been for Jeff . . .

I raced up the little hill.

"Thank you," I whined. Wiggling and waggling all over, I jumped up and put my front paws on his chest. "Thank you for coming after me. They were going to eat me. Thank you, thank you, thank you."

"Get down." He shoved me away. I could tell by the tone of his voice and his smile that he really didn't mean it. So I jumped up to thank him again. "What in the world's wrong with you, T.P.? I know chasing deer is exciting. But you're a *bird* dog, remember? And you're supposed to come when I whistle. Get your tail on to the house. It's cold out here."

The chill of the morning really didn't bother me. Not until I got to thinking about what a close call I'd had with those nasty coyotes. By the time we got to the house, I had the shivers.

The second Jeff opened the door, I darted inside. Daddy had a fire going in the fireplace. I loved to lie on the mat in front of the hearth and soak up the warmth.

I went straight there, nestled down on the mat, and curled into a ball. This was wonderful. Warm and cozy. Safe. Comfortable. Quiet and peaceful and—

"Yipe. Yipe."

My eyes popped wide. My head snapped up.

Cord raced through the playroom doorway.

"No!" Jeff yelled. "Puppy. Stop!"

Cord's claws frantically scraped the linoleum floor, only he wasn't going anywhere. The puppy was almost to him when he finally got some traction, flew across the floor, and headed for the dining room table.

The puppy's claws slipped on the smooth floor. Eyes wide and tongue dangling out the side of its mouth, the thing spun and slipped, trying to catch the flying cat.

Cord leaped. I flinched.

Then, to my surprise, he made it. He

actually leaped for the table and made it. Landed right on the thing . . .

Only he was going too fast. He slid. The tablecloth slid. Mama and Daddy's coffee cups slid. The fake flowers in the middle of the table slid.

Eyes wide, all Jeff and I could do was watch as Cord, coffee cups, and flowers slid clear to the far side of the table.

Right at the edge, everything stopped. I held my breath.

Cord's tail swooped in a couple of wide, jerky circles as he tried to get his balance. Then . . .

The whole thing went.

The cat crashed. The tablecloth crashed. The coffee cups and the fake flowers crashed.

The noise startled the puppy. Right at the edge of the carpet, it put on the brakes. Jeff was running so fast, trying to catch it, he couldn't stop. He tripped over the puppy. And . . . sure enough . . .

Jeff crashed, too.

Did I say our home was quiet and peaceful?

Chapter 7

Our home *was* quiet and peaceful.

Once Jeff put the puppy outside.

Mama and Daddy came to the playroom door to see what had happened. Jeff bent over and picked up their coffee cups. On the way to the sink, he paused to smile at them.

"They didn't break. I'll wash them for you after I get the coffee off the carpet and put the tablecloth in the washer, okay?"

Shaking her head, Mama rushed over and gathered the tablecloth in her arms. "I'll take care of the tablecloth," she called. "You just get a pan of soapy water and work on the carpet." She paused again at the hallway. "Make sure it's *cold* water, Jeff."

"Yes, ma'am," he shouted back.

"What in the world was that?" Cord meowed.

He was peeking from behind the couch. His eyes were wide and his whiskers stuck straight out.

"A puppy."

Cord eased a bit farther from his hiding place.

"A puppy? You mean like you were when you first came here?"

My head snapped straight up.

"Definitely not! I was *never* that wild and crazy. I didn't chase you. Besides that, I didn't leak."

"Beg your pardon," Cord said with a flip of his tail. "The first couple of days you were here, you were pretty wild. After that, you just slept most of the time. And the only reason you didn't chase me was because I swatted you on the nose the first time you tried. And as far as leaking . . ." Head tilted way to the side, he paused a moment, as if trying to remember. "Okay. You didn't leak. But you did have a couple of accidents."

I gave a little snort. Crouched low, Cord peeked around the corner of the coffee table. "Where is the little—"

There was a loud *KERTHUNK* when the puppy bounced against the back door. From the corner of my eye, all I could see was a dark streak as Cord flew behind the couch once more.

"It's outside, Cord," I told him. "Just relax a little."

Cord's whiskers appeared at the side of the couch. "You sure?"

"Yeah. Jeff put it out. By the way, why did you run from it? You never ran from me."

The cat eased around the corner, then hopped up on the coffee table. He took a long look around to make sure I hadn't lied to him about the puppy being outside. Finally he flipped his tail and sat down.

"Thing took me totally by surprise," Cord admitted. "One minute I was snoozing away on the back of the couch. The next, there was a cold, wet nose stuck in my ear. When I opened my eyes, here was this huge, brown, fuzzy monster looking at me. Then it licked me—right across the face." He shrugged his whiskers. "I didn't even suspect it was a dog until it barked. By then it was too late. I was all fuzzed up and halfway to the table."

Jeff set a plastic pan on the floor. He knelt beside it and started rubbing at the carpet with a wet cloth.

"Where did it come from? And what's it doing in our house?" Cord asked.

I cocked an ear, pointing at Jeff. "Jeff's friend left it early this morning. She's gone on vacation or something. Don't worry, though. Mama told Jeff the girl has to take it home when she gets back."

"Yeah. Right." Cord's tail flipped.

"What does that mean?" I frowned.

Cord arched an eyebrow. "I didn't figure you'd last long around here, either. You've been here four years, now."

"But that's what Mama told him."

"You know how softhearted she is." Cord sighed. "Just wait. You'll see."

My head sank to the floor and rested on

top of my crossed paws. Man, that was a horrible thought. What if the puppy stayed? What if . . .

Jeff finished scrubbing the carpet. He took the pan and cloth to the kitchen. Mama came back from the laundry room. For a moment I thought about joining the three of them in the playroom, but the hearth was just too warm and comfortable. So I laid my head on the carpet and closed my eyes.

I hadn't even had a chance to doze when Jeff whistled. Instantly I hopped up and trotted over to see what he wanted. Jeff patted a place beside him on the couch. I curled up with my head on the padded arm and my rump against his leg.

"I'll get the cat," Mama said.

"I'll get the puppy." Daddy had a rope in his hand.

Something was going on. I wasn't sure whether I liked the sound of this or not.

Mama came back with Cord in her arms. Only she didn't hold on to him. She set him on the other side of Jeff.

"Don't try to hold the cat," Mama warned.

Jeff nodded.

The puppy came into the playroom, dragging Daddy. It coughed and gagged and choked because it was leaning so hard against the rope on its neck. Daddy closed the door behind him and bent down.

The puppy was loose!

I felt my shoulders tense. Sure enough, here it came.

Normal dog introductions consist of a slow approach, easing closer and closer until you can smell and sense how the other dog feels about your presence. Then there's posturing—trying to look big and impressive if it's another boy dog. Or trying to look handsome and strong if it's a girl dog. Then there's lots of sniffing—the way we really communicate and get to know each other.

Trouble was, there was nothing normal about this puppy. The thing flew right up in my face. Sniffed so hard it almost pulled my whiskers into its nose.

I bared my teeth. "Back off, Bozo," I growled deep in my throat.

Jeff leaned over and patted me on the head. "Take it easy, T.P. She's just saying hello." His pat was really more of a "shove my head down" than a pat.

I growled again. The puppy got out of my face long enough for me to take a quick sniff.

Bird dogs have a great sense of smell. From just one little snort, I could tell the puppy was a girl. She was kind and had a sweet disposition. And . . .

She was TOTALLY hyper!

In the blink of an eye, she was back in my face again.

"Hi. What's your name? I don't have a name. Mother said I have to wait until my people give me a name.

"Are you a dog? I'm a dog. I'm a chocolate Labrador retriever.

"Do you know what retrievers are? I don't. But Mother said that's what we are.

"Are you a dog? You smell like a dog. You kind of look like a dog, only not as big or pretty as my mother.

"Are these your people? Are they going to be my people? I hope so. They seem really nice.

"What's your name?"

My eyes crossed as I looked down the tip of my nose at her. I'd never heard so many questions. It seemed like thousands of them, coming out of nowhere, one right after the other.

She was crowding me again. I curled my lips back so she could see how long and sharp my teeth were. I didn't get a chance to growl.

"Oh," she yapped. "There's that strange animal again." She stumbled over Jeff's feet, trying to get to the other end of the couch. "What are you? I'm a puppy. I don't have a name."

Cord's tail jerked one way, then the other. When the puppy stretched up for a closer sniff, he hopped to his feet. His tail puffed.

Watch it! That cat's got a wicked right hook. I thought it, but I sure didn't say it out loud. I figured this pup was going to have to learn things the hard way.

Sure enough, Cord was so quick he hit her with three left jabs and a right hook before she even had time to yank her head back.

All I could do was smile.

Chapter 8

"Have you seen my ball? I can't find my ball. Do you know what I did with my ball?"

Her head jerked and her ears flopped, then she spotted it in front of the TV. She bounded over and picked it up—but came right back.

"Why do they call you T.P.?

"Why do they call the cat Cord?

"What is a cat, anyway? Is it sort of like a dog, only different?

"How did he get such sharp claws? I can't believe how quick he hits.

"Can you believe how quick he hits?

"What do you think they'll name me?

"Will they give me a name soon?

"When did they give you your name?

"Want to play chase?

"Huh? Huh?

"You want to?"

Four days of this one-question-after-another stuff was really getting on my nerves. I bared my teeth.

"Don't you ever shut up?" I snapped. "I didn't know dogs could talk that fast. I've never even heard people talk as fast as you do. You're driving me nuts."

"What are nuts? Are they animals?

"Why do you lie on the couch? Is the couch softer than the floor? Why do they call it the couch?"

"SHUT UP!" I roared.

Her floppy ears flattened against the side of her head, and her tail drooped—but for only a second. Then her ears arched again.

"Okay." She smiled.

With that, the puppy trotted over to the front of the TV. She curled up and started chewing on her rubber ball with the little jingly bell inside.

I flopped my head down so hard, the whole couch shook. Mama was in the kitchen. She peeked around the corner of the playroom.

"T.P., be nice to the puppy."

I wagged my tail. But as soon as Mama turned her back, my lip curled. "Be nice to the puppy," I snarled. "That's all I ever hear."

My only hope was that Saturday would get here soon, and Jeff's friend would come and take this mutt away. Only trouble was, I didn't know when Saturday was. I knew it was a day that Mama, Daddy, and Jeff got to stay home. But this was Spring Break. Jeff and Mama were home all week. All I could do was keep my paws crossed and hope Saturday would hurry.

I didn't even get a quick snooze before something jarred my couch. My head snapped up. Blinking, I looked around to see what it was.

The puppy leaped at the far end of my couch. Shook the cushion with her paws as she tried to jump up. Her short legs were the only thing that saved me. After four or five tries, she finally figured out she couldn't make it.

"How do you get up there?

"Do you have a special trick? I want up there, too. Can you teach me?

"What's Mama doing in the kitchen?

"Why do we call her Mama? She's not my mother. Is she your mother?

"Why does that big box, with the light inside, make so much noise all the time?

"Why do the people sit and stare at it so much?"

"KNOCK IT OFF!"

Suddenly realizing how loudly I'd barked, I knew Mama would be coming to check. Instantly I flopped my head on the couch and covered my eye with an ear. Maybe Mama would think I was asleep. Maybe she'd decide she just thought she'd heard something.

Her footsteps made sounds as she walked from the sink to the doorway. I didn't move. The sounds stopped. Behind my ear I could almost see her standing there, frowning at me. I held my breath. After a time the sound of footsteps moved back into the kitchen.

"Are you asleep? I think you're just playing like you're asleep. Are you playing?"

I moved my ear. The puppy stood there, ears cocked and nose not even an inch from mine.

"Get out of my face."

"I'm not on your face. I'm standing right here. See?"

"Back off!"

"Why don't you like me?"

I raised my head and looked down my

nose at her. Her brown eyes were sad. Her tail drooped and the corners of her mouth sagged.

"Look, kid. It's not that I don't like you. You're just a total pest. You ask a million and one questions. You keep getting in my face and—"

"What's a pest? I'm a chocolate Lab. I'm not a pest. And you never answer my questions. Why don't you answer when I ask you something?"

I snapped my teeth at her—not loud enough for Mama to hear—but enough to get her attention.

"*And,*" I snarled, "you're always interrupting."

"But why won't you answer my questions? Maybe if you talked to me I wouldn't have so many questions."

"The reason I don't answer"—I sighed—"is because you never give me a chance."

She blinked and her little head kind of snapped back. "I don't?"

"You don't. You spew out four or five questions before I even have a chance to think."

"If I just ask one, will you answer?"

My tail thumped the cushion. "You can't do it."

"Can't do what? Ask one question? I think I can. Don't you think I can? What makes you think—"

"See."

She paused a moment, frowning. "Okay, okay." She sat down and took a deep breath.

I arched an ear. Waited. And waited.

"Well?"

She stood up again and leaned toward me. "I don't know what to ask. There are so many things I need to find out. I don't know where to start."

"First, start by getting your nose out of my face. Your smeller works just fine. You don't have to stand so close."

"Oh. Okay. Sorry. Just one question? Can't I have more than one? Huh? Please? Pretty please?"

When I sighed, my whiskers wiggled. "Tell you what. I'll make a deal with you. You can have three questions, IF you'll go lie down and be quiet until Jeff comes to feed us. Deal?"

She hopped to her feet and wagged her tail. "You promise?"

"I promise."

"Okay. Deal." Then her eyebrows scrunched down and her tongue stuck out the corner of her mouth. "I want to ask when I get my name. I want to know how I get my name, too. Mother said that people give us our names. Sometimes they name us for things we do, or for our color, or after other dogs they once had." She talked to herself, instead of to me. So I just waited. "But since the people do that stuff, you probably wouldn't be able to tell me.

"And . . . I want to know how you get up on the couch, and I want to know what a cat is, and how the cat got his name, and why everyone calls the woman Mama when she's not our Mama and . . . and . . ." Head hung low, she sighed.

I nestled my cheek into the throw pillow at the end of the couch. This was working pretty well, I thought. She's so busy trying to think what to ask, I'm at least getting a few minutes' rest.

Suddenly her head snapped. Her eyes sparkled.

"Okay. I've got it. I've got my first question. Since you don't know when I'll get my name or how they will name me . . . Here goes. What does T.P. mean, and how did they name you?"

"That's two questions."

"Wait. Wait. Don't answer." Her tongue stuck out the corner of her mouth. She kind of nibbled on it, thinking. "Okay, I've got it. *Why* did they name you T. P.?"

My eyes rolled. The air kind of whooshed out of me. "Ask something else, kid. I really don't want to—"

"You promised."

My eyes narrowed when I glared at her. Then I slumped into the throw pillow and sighed.

"You're right. I promised."

Chapter 9

Sometimes Jeff would promise me we were going quail hunting. I spent the whole day thinking about the wonderful smell of those birds, and how exciting it was to follow them until they huddled together and didn't move. Then Jeff would come closer. Suddenly they would burst into the air—fluttering, flying, going every which way. It was exciting. Chasing them and trying to find where they landed was ten times more fun than chasing a rabbit.

But sometimes—not very often, just sometimes—things would happen and Jeff would break his promise. We wouldn't go.

Having a promise broken always made me feel sad.

"Okay," I said, looking the puppy square

in the eye. "They call me T.P.," I began, "because one time when I was a puppy . . ."

I told her all about discovering a piece of paper hanging beside the tall, white drinking bowl in the bathroom. It looked like something to chew on, but when I reached up to get it, it held on to its friends. Other pieces started to follow. Holding it in my mouth, all the others came, too. Fluttering and sailing along behind me, they chased me all through the house. It was fun

watching the paper float and wave as I raced across the living room, around the chair, and down the hall.

When the people found all the paper, they made mean mouth noises at me. But they also laughed and chuckled. It was a little confusing. So I figured they weren't really mad. Besides, it was a whole lot of fun to race through the house with the white banner following me. The next day I did it again. After the fourth time, they really *were* mad. So I didn't do it anymore.

I explained that the rolled-up paper was toilet paper. Sometimes it was just called T.P. That's how I got my name.

Next she asked how Cord got his name.

I told her it was short for *coordination*.

Cord didn't have any.

She had no idea what it meant, so I explained that, basically, most cats were graceful and very good at leaping and catching prey. In other words, their eyes and nose and senses all worked together.

But this cat was clumsy. It wasn't really his fault, though. Cord was cross-eyed. That made it hard for him to judge distances and jump from one place to another. There were even times when he was just running through the house and would end up slamming into stuff or bouncing off a wall or chair.

"Last question," I said sternly.

She lowered her head, stared at the floor for a moment, then looked at me.

"Will you be my friend?"

What kind of question is that? I thought. She's only going to be here a few more days. She's hyper and halfway crazy— always running through the house, chewing on that stupid ball, and yapping at Cord. She has no manners and asks a million stupid questions. Then she wants to know if I'll be her friend.

The puppy didn't raise her head. She just watched me. Kind of stared out of the top of those big, sad, brown eyes. I didn't know what to say.

"My brothers and sisters all went away with their people. I miss them. Mandy played with me and was nice to me. Then she put me in a box and brought me here. I miss my mother. I'm lonely. Have you ever been lonely? I really want you to be my friend. Please."

A little twinge hit me. It was down deep inside. I'm not sure where it came from. For an instant I remembered playing with my brothers and sisters. Mother was gentle with us. She was so soft. I felt safe with her.

Then Jeff and Daddy took me and brought me here. I cried the first night because I was so scared and lonely. But Jeff loved me and played with me. Mama and Daddy loved me, too. This is where I belonged, and it was hardly any time at all before they made me forget the lonely. Still . . .

This was my home. Jeff was my boy. This was my yard and my couch and . . .

But lonely . . . well, lonely is just . . . lonely.

I sighed, plopped my head on the pillow, and closed my eyes.

"Sure, kid. I'll be your friend." Then I raised my head and glared down my nose at her. "But you've got to behave yourself.

You've got to calm down a little and not act so wild. And . . . and . . . and that was your last question. Now shut up and let me rest until Jeff feeds us."

Smiling from ear to ear and tail fanning the breeze, she didn't ask one more single question. That sort of surprised me. She just trotted over, picked up her ball, and started chewing on it.

My luck was running true to form. I'd just nestled my head into the pillow when I heard the frantic scratching sound of claws scraping on top of the piano.

I squeezed my eyes shut and gritted my teeth, because I *knew* what would come next.

There would be more scratching, followed by a C-minor or an F-sharp chord from the piano keys (depending on whether Cord landed on his side or his bottom), followed finally by a loud *Kerthunk* when he hit the floor.

It was a C-minor chord (that meant he landed on his side), then the *Kerthunk!*

Once the racket was over, I raised my head and looked.

Cord flipped his tail and strutted away from the piano, as if nothing had happened.

Something brushed my whiskers. I glanced to the side. The puppy was so close to my nose, it was hard to see her.

"What was that terrible sound?" she asked, wide-eyed as could be. "What happened?"

Then she spotted Cord, and started toward him.

"Wait!" I whispered. "He just fell off the piano. Don't bother him right now—he'll rip you to shreds."

"Does that happen a lot?"

I shrugged my eyebrows. "Yeah. But just go lie down and pretend nothing happened."

She paused a second, then went back to chew on her ball.

After breakfast, there were three more questions. The puppy was hyper and wild, but she wasn't totally stupid. She chose her questions carefully. How do you get on the couch? What is a cat? And . . . Well, I can't remember her last one. Then she left me alone for a good hour before she came back with three more.

Way I had it figured, it wouldn't hurt to be nice to her. Aside from her bounce and wiggle and million and one questions, she did have a sweet disposition.

Besides, Saturday couldn't be that far away.

That afternoon Jeff took us out in the back-yard. The snow was already gone, even in the shade. He spent a long time staring down at the giant drinking bowl. The water looked a little clearer now, instead of totally green and yucky. Jeff loved to play in the giant drinking bowl. Every year he could hardly wait to help Daddy take off the cover.

When he knelt on one knee and reached in, I scampered over to see what he was after. Jeff wasn't reaching for anything. He just stuck his hand in and yanked it right back out. Then he shook the water off.

"Needs a couple more days. Still cold as ice." He pouted. Then he rubbed me behind the ears. "How about a walk, T.P.? You ready to go?"

The walk was GREAT! I got to run and smell. I even found a couple of quail, who flew away when I pointed them.

And, best of all, I got to do all that on my own.

The puppy's short little legs couldn't handle the tall grass in the pasture. So she stayed with Jeff on the road behind our house.

Jeff whistled when it was almost dark. I found him and led the way back to the house. Jeff carried the puppy in his arms. At first I thought she was just being lazy and trying to get a free ride. But when we got back to the house, she flopped in front of the TV and fell fast asleep. She didn't even bother to chew on her ball with the jingly thing inside.

She slept until well after dark. When

Mandy didn't show up, I figured out that it must not be Saturday yet.

After an hour or two, the puppy woke up. She came over to where I was relaxing, next to Mama, on the couch.

"First question." She grinned and wagged her tail. "Why do you leave the road to run, when it's much easier to walk on the—"

Suddenly she stopped. I guess she hadn't noticed Mama sitting next to me. Her tail waved back and forth so hard, it knocked some of the papers off the coffee table. She hopped up and put her front paws on Mama's knee.

With a smile, Mama leaned down and swooped her up. To my surprise, instead of jumping all around and trying to lick Mama in the face, the puppy curled up in Mama's lap. Mama petted her. The puppy nestled her cheek and rubbed it back and forth on Mama's tummy. She had the sweetest, happiest, most sickening look on her little puppy face that I'd ever seen.

Mama looked down at her.

When I saw the expression on Mama's face—when I felt the love that came from her—the peace and happiness . . .

With that one look, I realized that Saturday might *never* come.

Chapter 10

Saturday came.

I could tell it was Saturday because Mama smelled sad. Saturday meant that Spring Break was almost over and she had to go back to school. She usually smelled the same on the Fourth of July, too. The Fourth of July meant that summer was half over.

Jeff smelled excited and nervous. He kept staring at the ringie-thingie on the wall. Sometimes when it jingled, he could talk to Mandy. Then he went to the front door and looked out.

All the signs were there. All we needed now was for Mandy and her parents to come and take the puppy back home.

The ringie-thingie finally jingled. Mama

was in the kitchen. Jeff was at the front door. Even though the thing hung on the kitchen wall, Jeff beat her to it.

"Sure, we're up and dressed," Jeff told the little white thing. "Twenty minutes? Yeah, that would be fine. See you then."

Jeff put the ringie-thingie back on the wall. The moment he did, all three of my people went flying through the house to put their clothes on.

Wagging my tail, I stood beside Jeff and watched out the front screen. The magic gate swung open. But it was quite a while before a car came through and drove up our road. I barked to let my people know someone was coming. Jeff shushed me.

Mandy and her parents got out and walked to the door. Mama greeted them with smiles and mouth noises. Daddy was in the kitchen, fixing another pot of coffee.

When the puppy spotted Mandy, she jumped up and down and wiggled and ran all over the living room.

She leaked, too.

Jeff and Mandy took her outside. In a little bit they came back and joined the grown-ups around the dining room table. I lay at Jeff's feet. The puppy got to lie on Mandy's lap.

"This is great coffee," Mandy's daddy told Daddy. "What kind is it?"

"It's called Mocha Java."

Jeff frowned. "What does that mean, Dad?"

Daddy frowned. Then he shrugged. "I don't know. It's just coffee."

"I think Java is an island in the Pacific Ocean," Mama spoke up.

"Mocha is a chocolate, isn't it?" Mandy's mama added.

"I think so," Mama answered. Then she leaned across the table to look at Jeff. "Go get the dictionary."

Jeff's shoulders sagged. "That's the trouble with having a teacher for a mother," he whispered to Mandy. "They're always making you look up stuff."

Jeff trotted off to his room. I started to follow, but I was pretty sure he was coming right back. In a moment or two, he returned with a book. He sat down and started shuffling through the papers.

"Okay. 'Java: an island of Indonesia.' Number two says, 'coffee.'"

Mama smiled at Mandy's mama. "Means both, I guess. Coffee and the island."

Jeff rattled some more of the pages.

"'Mocha: a superior Arabian coffee consisting of small green or yellowish beans. Also a mixture of cocoa or chocolate with coffee.' And number two says, 'a pliable suede-finished glove leather from African sheepskins.'"

"Don't notice any chocolate flavor." Mandy's daddy smiled. "Just good old regular coffee. Must be the Arabian thing. Whatever it is, it's sure good."

Mandy sat up very straight and fluttered her eyes at Jeff. "I like that," she said. "Why don't we name our dogs Mocha and Java? You want to?"

Jeff shrugged. "Sure."

"Okay." Mandy's eyelashes fluttered once more. She stroked the puppy's back. "You name her Mocha. I'll name mine Java."

After more visiting and mouth noises, Jeff and Mandy slipped out the back door. I went with them. Whatever they were

going to do was probably a lot more interesting than listening to the grown-ups.

I went to sniff the pine tree while they walked around the giant drinking bowl.

"Let's go swimming," Jeff said.

Mandy crinkled her nose. "I didn't bring my bathing suit."

"Mama's got an extra one. It's a two-piece that's too small for her. It would probably be a little big on you, but you could wear it."

Mandy shot him a disgusted look and shook her head. "It's too cold."

"No, it's not," Jeff argued.

Mandy knelt on one knee and stuck her hand in the water. She yanked it out, really quick.

"It's like ice."

"Oh, you're just a sissy," Jeff scoffed.

Mandy threw a handful of water at him. She'd barely gotten to her feet when Jeff grabbed her by the shoulders and shoved her toward the drinking bowl. She squealed and wrapped her arms around his waist.

For an instant it scared me. What if Mandy fell into the water and couldn't get out? What if Jeff didn't know how to save her with the blue net like Daddy saved me? What if both of them . . .

Then I wasn't scared anymore.

I could tell by watching them that they were just playing. Since they were busy wrestling, there was no one for me to play with. Then the back door opened. Mama shoved the puppy outside. "She wants to be with you two," Mama called. "She needs some play time."

The puppy ran to them. She wiggled and waggled and squirmed and leaked when they petted her. She even dropped her ball so she could lick them. It was disgusting. So I went to see if there was a sparrow I could scare out of the pine tree.

A loud splash stopped me. The puppy was gone.

All at once Jeff rushed toward the water. He dropped to his knees and reached for something—only catching his balance at the last second before he toppled over.

"Jeff. Jeff." Mandy's voice was calm. "She's okay, Jeff."

But Jeff wasn't listening. He stood and kicked his shoes off.

"She's fine, Jeff," Mandy assured him. "That's what she's supposed to do. Jeff? Jeff!"

Clothes and all, Jeff jumped into the giant drinking bowl.

The spray shot high into the air. He bobbed back to the surface and let out a scream that sent the hair bristling up my back. It sounded like he needed help. My tail froze in mid-swing. My ears arched. My eyes popped wide. The scream scared me. But I hated to get too near the giant drinking bowl. So I raced to the back door. With a deep breath, I started barking so Daddy would come outside and save Jeff with the blue net.

Mandy folded her arms and cocked her head to one side. "Thought you told me it wasn't cold." She smiled. "You called me a sissy when I didn't want to go swimming."

A spray of water flew from the giant drinking bowl. Mandy jumped back. She stood on her tiptoes. "Don't lift her out," she called. "She's doing fine. Just guide her to the steps."

The door swung open behind me. Daddy leaned out. "What's all the racket about?" he asked, glaring down at me.

I ran toward the giant drinking bowl. "Jeff screamed!" I barked. When Daddy didn't follow, I raced back to him. "He must have fallen into the giant drinking bowl. He never goes in with all his clothes on," I barked. "You have to help him. Please. Save Jeff!"

Chapter 11

I couldn't believe it! Daddy ignored me. He didn't come running to save our Jeff. He didn't grab the blue net with the long handle. He just stood there.

"Mandy," he called. "What's going on?"

She glanced over her shoulder. "Oh, Jeff accidentally kicked the ball into the pool. The pup went after it, and Jeff thinks he has to save her."

Mandy's daddy shoved his way out the door, and stood beside Daddy—but neither of them raced to save Jeff. Then the two mamas appeared behind them.

"Jeff!" Mandy's daddy called.

Jeff's head appeared above the side of the drinking bowl. He had the pup in his arm. She was still paddling for all she was worth. "Yes, sir," he answered.

"Let her swim with the ball. Just guide her to the steps so she can get out and not scratch the liner."

"Okay."

Jeff disappeared. In a moment, I saw the puppy. A second later Jeff's head appeared near the wide end of the drinking bowl. Then he stood up and I saw his shoulders, then his chest. A sigh of relief whooshed out of me when I knew he was safe.

The puppy swam along with Jeff following her. Every now and then Jeff kind of nudged her rump, first in one direction and then the other. Near the very edge of the drinking bowl, where the silver pole is, she suddenly stood up. She hopped over the side and shook. Tiny droplets sprayed in all directions. Then, wagging her tail, she raced to Mandy and dropped the ball at her feet.

"Water a little cold, son?" Daddy smiled.

Jeff shivered. "Was at first. But I'm getting used to it."

Jeff was lying. His teeth clattered together as fast and loud as a woodpecker tapping on a tree. Besides that, his lips were kind of purple.

"If you can stand it a few more minutes," Mandy's daddy said, "it takes them about three or four times to learn where the steps are. You game?"

"Yes, sir." Jeff's teeth chattered. "I'm doing fine."

Jeff pulled his sweatshirt over his head and threw it at Mandy. She jumped out of the way and stuck her tongue out at him. "Just for that, I think I'll throw it in the deep end."

Mandy's daddy nodded. She threw the ball again. She didn't throw it in the deep end like she threatened. She tossed it just a few feet from where Jeff stood shivering.

I couldn't believe my eyes!

The crazy pup tore off after that ball. At the edge of the giant drinking bowl, she leaped. She was more than halfway to Jeff when she hit the water. Spray flew. Her face went clear under when she snapped at the ball.

Again she dropped it at Mandy's feet. Eyes wide, tail wagging, hopping up and down, she could hardly wait for Mandy to throw it a second time.

She did.

Crazy mutt raced to the edge and flew through the air. When she tried to swim back to Mandy, Jeff caught up with her and shoved her in the right direction. The next time she went after the ball, he had to guide her again. After that, she went where she was supposed to.

"Is Jeff doing okay?" Mandy's daddy asked.

Daddy smiled and nodded. "He thinks we're supposed to open the pool the first day of spring—no matter what the temperature is. And if there's any sunshine, he thinks he's supposed to start swimming. Doesn't matter how cold. He's been like that ever since we put the pool in. How about the pup?"

Mandy's daddy smiled back at him.

"She's fine. Labs have that real tight layer of short, fine hair next to their skin. Doesn't make 'em waterproof, but serves as an extra insulation barrier. Guarantee you that dog doesn't even feel the cold."

As far as I was concerned, that puppy was downright crazy. Just watching her leap, again and again, into the cold water was enough to give me the shivers.

I'd had my suspicions about the puppy all along. Now I knew. She was totally bonkers—loony—crazy as a bed bug.

When Jeff started turning blue all over, Mama made him get out. She gave him a towel. He rubbed himself with it and went to put on some dry clothes. She brought another towel, and helped Mandy dry the puppy off.

Once back inside the house, I curled up in front of the fireplace. The fact that there wasn't a fire didn't bother me. It still seemed like the warmest place I could find. Wrapped in the towel, the puppy fell fast asleep in Mandy's arms.

How many times they'd thrown that ball in the pool, I couldn't remember. Every time she had dropped it at Mandy's feet, she'd hardly been able to stand still. She was so excited and ready to go again, all she did was watch the ball, watch Mandy, and wiggle all over. The look in her soft brown eyes was totally wild—like that ball was the only thing in the world and diving in the water to get it was the most important thing in her whole life.

Like I said, CRAZY!

Mama and Daddy invited Mandy and her parents to stay for lunch. The men went into the playroom and turned on the TV. The women went to the kitchen and started rattling pots and pans. Keeping an eye on where the grown-ups went, Mandy and Jeff sat with the puppy on the couch and petted it.

I closed my eyes. I felt them roll around inside my head when I remembered the night I saw Mama holding that stupid puppy. She petted her and smiled down at her. I had a bad feeling even then. I just knew . . .

Man, I hated being right.

Saturday came and went.

The puppy didn't went.

The puppy stayed.

Chapter 12

"Where's my ball?

"Have you seen my ball? I can't remember what I did with it. Oh, there it is.

"Why do they keep yelling Mocha at me?

"What's a Mocha?

"Why does Jeff always say, 'Tee tee, puppy,' when he puts me out the front door?

"Is that my name?

"Are you trying to sleep? I'm sorry. I didn't know you were trying to sleep. Are you asleep?

"You want to play?

"Huh? Huh?

"You want to?"

"GEERRRRR!"

"T.P.," Mama called from the other room. "Be nice to the puppy. I mean Mocha."

"Why does Jeff put that little white thing against the side of his head and talk to it?

"Why does he keep saying Mandy? It doesn't look like Mandy.

"Where *is* Mandy? I haven't seen her for a whole bunch of days.

"Will she come back?

"What does 'go for a walk' mean?"

My head popped from the couch cushion. I hopped off and trotted to the kitchen. Sure enough, Jeff leaned against the wall and smiled at the little white ringie-thingie that usually hung on the wall. He nodded his head, then shrugged.

"I don't know," he told it. "We could just walk around and explore. The ticks aren't out yet. I'd still wear jeans, though.

"Well, you wear whatever you want. I'm wearing my jeans.

"Okay. See you in a few minutes."

I followed him to his bedroom. He opened his closet and laid a clean pair of jeans and a nice shirt on the bed. He went to the bathroom next. I stayed with him while he washed his face. But when he started spraying that stinky stuff under his arms, it made me sneeze. I had to get out of there.

"T.P., knock it off," Daddy scolded when I trotted past on my way to the playroom. He looked at Mama and shook his head. "That's the sneezingest dog I ever saw in my life."

I still got in about three more before I could stop.

The puppy had told me Jeff used the words 'Go for a walk.' I didn't know whether I believed her or not. That's because when Jeff came to the playroom, he had on his good tennis shoes. When we went hunting, he always wore hunting boots. When we went 'Go for a walk,' he put on his grungy old tennis shoes.

Something was different. So instead of racing around the house and bouncing against the front door, I decided just to cool it. I waited on the couch to see what happened.

Jeff sat with us, but he didn't pay much

attention to the TV. Instead he kept hopping up to look out the window.

"Why is Jeff so nervous?

"Is he looking for his ball?

"Does he have a ball?

"Why does he keep jumping up and down?"

"*GEERRRRR!*"

"T.P., quit that," Jeff said, swooping the puppy up in his arms. As soon as he did, she nestled her head against his chest and looked up at him with those big brown eyes. "Mocha's such a sweet puppy. Yes. You're a good girl," he cooed. Then he frowned at me. "I don't know why you keep growling at her. Be nice."

It was sickening.

After a while, Jeff set Mocha on the floor. "Come on, T.P. Let's take her outside to tee-tee."

"He's doing it again," Mocha said. "Why does he keep calling me tee-tee puppy?

"Is that my name? I thought my name was Mocha.

"Is Mocha my name?

"What's my name?"

I heisted my leg on the sweet gum tree and headed to check out the fence line. Before I even got halfway across the yard, I heard a grinding sound. Eyes wide, I watched as the magic gate opened.

Jeff whistled. "Come back up here, T.P.," he called. "We'll go later. Stay close so Mocha can take care of business."

When she finally squatted in the grass, Jeff praised her, told her she was a good tee-tee puppy, and petted her. I heisted my leg on the tree again. He didn't even notice *me*. Then he let us inside, but he didn't follow.

In a few minutes, a car turned into our drive. Jeff rushed around the side of the house. Mama came to the front door. She shoved Mocha and me aside with her foot. "Hi, Barbara. Mandy." She frowned and looked past them. "Where's Art?"

"Last week when we were here, you and Ben fixed dinner for us. Art decided it was our turn. He's got a couple of errands to run, then he's going to stop by Roy's and pick up some barbecue. Is that okay?"

"Sounds great. Ben loves Roy's barbecue. All of us do."

Jeff leaned his head in. "Do we have time for a walk before we eat?"

Mama looked at Mandy's mama, who nodded. "Probably be about an hour before he gets here," Mandy's mama answered.

Mama turned to Jeff. "Sure. Don't get too far off."

"Yes, ma'am."

Jeff held the door wide, then whistled. I started out, but Mocha beat me to the opening. My legs were a lot longer, so I jumped over her and got back in front.

I raced for the fence line, to see if any new animals had been there during the night. Mocha followed, but when I squeezed under the barbed-wire fence and into the tall grass, she turned back.

"Finally!" I wagged. "Some peace and quiet."

Coyotes had been there. But the smells were old. Two rabbits. Fresh smells—from early this morning. A field mouse. Another rabbit and . . .

"Got it!"

I paused long enough to glance over my shoulder. Jeff had hold of the ball in Mocha's mouth. He had to wrestle her for it, but finally pulled it loose and wiped his hand on his jeans.

"She'd drop the thing while we're walking, and go totally crazy if she couldn't find it. Wait here. I'll run and put it in the house."

I sniffed around the plum patch, then glanced to see where they were again. Jeff and Mandy were strolling toward the creek.

A good bird dog stays in front of his people. That way we can show them where the birds are before they scare them away. Even though we weren't hunting for birds, that was my job. Ears flat and head low for speed, I raced to get ahead of them.

It was a wonderful morning for a run. There was still a chill in the early spring air. It felt crisp and clean. At the creek I checked carefully to make sure the coyotes weren't around. There was no scent of them. There was no smell of the giant rabbit I'd chased a few weeks ago, either.

At the edge of the forest, I kicked my nose into overdrive. There was no way I wanted to stumble onto those coyotes again.

With no smell of them, I raced down to the pond. Some tall wavy grass things stood at the edge of the water. Jeff called them cattails. It was shallow where they grew, and after all my running, I needed a drink.

I was almost to the water when a smell caught my nose. Stopping, I sniffed again. It was a bird smell. Not quail or meadow-lark or sparrow—it was a new smell. Something strange and different. But it was definitely a bird.

Moving slowly and carefully, I crept forward an inch at a time. I still couldn't find what belonged to the smell. Leaning over my front paws, I eased my head between some of the cattail blades. A few feet ahead of me, there was a pile of dry grass. It was round with more grass on the outside edges and lower toward the middle. I took another step.

There was something inside the circle of dry grass. Round things—about eight of them. They looked hard and they didn't move. I took another step.

"HOOOOOONK!"

My eyes sprang wide. I jumped. Water splashed. Cattails bent and rustled as something charged from them and came straight for me. It burst through the tall grass. My front legs backed up. But my hind legs forgot to move. I almost fell over them.

The thing was huge. It spread its wings. Now it was twice as big as me. A broad flat mouth shot toward me and nipped me on my right ear.

"Ouch!" I yelped, stumbling backward.

"HOOOOONK!" The enormous bird screamed again. "Get away from my nest!"

It didn't whistle or tweet like most birds. It said "honk." It was big. The biggest bird I ever saw in my life. It bit my ear. But . . .

It *was* a bird.

I was a bird dog. Birds run from bird dogs. *We* do not run from birds.

I turned to *walk* away.

The darned thing snapped me again. Got me right on the tip of my tail.

I took off for Jeff. My sore tail was tucked so far under my belly, the tip touched my chest. I ran as hard as I could go.

Chapter 13

It was downright embarrassing.

What made it even worse was the coyotes. I heard them giggling. It took a second or two to spot the scraggly things. They stood at the edge of some tangled briars, up the hill about forty yards from the pond. They pointed at me with their noses—and laughed and laughed.

I turned and moved on. About halfway to Jeff and Mandy I stopped, glancing back to make sure the huge bird wasn't following. The thing didn't look nearly as big with its back turned and its wings down by its sides. It waddled into the reeds. Far enough away that I was safe from another sneak attack, I finally recognized what the thing was.

It was a goose.

One time, when Jeff and I were both pretty small, Daddy had taken us to "The Park." We ran and played until I saw these birds near the pond. When I chased them, most said, "Quack!" They ran away. They flapped their wings and raced into the water. When they were out of my reach, I turned to chase another bird.

This bird didn't say "Quack." It said "HONK!" It didn't run away, either. It raced straight for me, clunked me with its wings and snapped me on the back with its big flat beak. When Jeff came to my rescue, the bird had attacked him, too.

Geese were mean. Geese didn't have any respect for anything or anyone. When Daddy came to save Jeff, the bird charged him. It had nipped Daddy—right on the bottom.

Still, it was embarrassing for a bird dog to run from a bird. Forcing my tail from under my belly, I inspected it.

No blood. No tooth marks. It still tingled a bit, right at the very tip where the thing had snapped me. I kicked the dirt with my hind paws.

I ought to go back. I ought to show it who's boss. I ought to . . .

Another head poked from the reeds. Snaking out at the end of a long neck, it had angry eyes and a big flat mouth. The eyes were small and beady. They glared at me.

There were two geese!

I snorted and kicked the grass again.

Okay—I'd go see what Jeff was doing.

A dead tree lay on its side near the corner of the dam. Jeff and Mandy were sitting on it.

I never got the chance to tell them about the giant birds.

Mocha spotted me. Eyes wide and tongue dangling out the side of her mouth, she charged down the bank.

"Is this another giant drinking bowl?" she panted. "Are they going to throw my ball?

"Where's my ball?

"Did they bring my ball?"

"This is not a drinking bowl," I snarled, lifting my head high so she couldn't lick my face. "This is a pond. They left your ball at the—"

"Where do you go when you leave us?" she interrupted. "Do you play with another dog?

"Do you find something to eat?

"Are there neat places to explore?

"How do you find your way back? I can't see over that tall grass.

"Can you see over the grass?

"Why do—"

"GEERRRRR!" I snapped at her face, but I didn't bite her.

"T.P., quit that!" Jeff called from the fallen log. "Be nice to Mocha."

I wagged my tail. "Only three questions," I growled softly, turning my attention back to Mocha. "Three, remember. And you wait for me to answer before you . . ."

She was gone.

I looked all around to see where she went. Head high and nose popping to sniff the breeze, she scampered off down the bank.

I looked up, too. But I didn't see anything except blue sky. Crazy little mutt, I thought, shaking my head. That pup has the attention span of a gnat. With a shrug of my ears, I trotted on to see what Jeff was doing.

Jeff and Mandy weren't doing anything exciting. At least, not as far as I could tell. They just sat on the log and made people noises. This was boring.

A whooshing sound made my ears perk up. I looked around. There was nothing there. Tilting my head to the side, I listened. The sound came from above. I looked up. The bright sunshine made me blink.

From the corner of my eye, I caught a movement. It was one of the huge birds that had chased me from the cattails. The goose soared high above the pond. Even as far away as he was, with his wings spread wide he looked enormous. There was something in his mouth. I had to squint, but I finally spotted some pieces of dry grass or straw. He tipped a wing and circled, again, lower this time.

I propped my paws up next to Jeff on the log. "Let's do something," I said in my best whine. "Let's go explore some other place. You and Mandy are just sitting there."

Jeff didn't hear me, I guess. So I put my paws on his leg, and shook him. Not even looking, he shoved me away.

"Humph," I snorted. "I'll just go explore by myself."

The far side of the dam would probably be a good place. I decided to check where the coyotes were before I started off. Not wanting people to see them, they were just sitting by the briars, smirking at me.

I was still watching when something floated between us. Wings spread wide, one of the geese glided just above the water. Then he reached out with his feet. Only his feet didn't look like bird feet. Instead of scaly little fingers with claws at the end, his feet were wide and flat. And instead of reaching for a limb to grab hold of, he was reaching for the water. I couldn't imagine how he was going to grab the water and hold on, with those big flat feet.

Feet touched first, but they didn't grab the water. They stayed flat, skidding across the surface just as smooth and slick as my paws skidded on ice. Spray arched out. Two V-shaped trails followed him across the pond. After a ways, he slowed and started to sink. Wings folding along his sides, he settled into the water.

I felt sorry for him.

Remembering the giant drinking bowl, I knew how scary it was to fall in the water and . . .

Only he didn't sink. He didn't flop around or try to climb out. He just floated. Gliding as smooth as Mama's touch when she stroked my back, he sailed toward the cattails.

SPLASH!

The sudden sound snapped my head around so fast, my ears flopped. Then my eyes flashed. I guess I expected to see the other big bird coming to greet him. The sound didn't come from a bird.

It was Mocha!

She swam for all she was worth—straight for the enormous bird.

"That's not your ball," I woofed. "Get back up here. That thing's mean. Leave him alone."

Eyes wild and tongue dangling out the side of her mouth, she paddled faster than I'd ever seen her swim before. The goose didn't try to get away. In fact, it swam straight for her.

"Oh, my gosh." I heard Mandy's voice behind me. "Mocha! No. Come back here!"

I glanced over my shoulder. Jeff was still sitting on the log. Mandy left him and ran down the bank toward me. She kept shouting, "No, Mocha! No!"

"Mandy. What's wrong?" Jeff sprang to his feet and chased after her. "What is it?"

"It's Mocha!" Now she was screaming instead of shouting. Her voice was high and scared. "She's in the water. She's trying to retrieve that goose. Mocha, come back here! That thing will drown her."

They were right beside me when Jeff finally caught up with Mandy. He grabbed hold of her shoulders and turned her.

"She'll be all right, Mandy," he soothed. "Soon as she sees how big it is, she'll turn around and—"

"No she won't," Mandy whimpered. "That's what she's bred for. She'll keep after it until it kills her. Help her. Please help her."

Mouth wide, Mocha reached out to catch the huge bird—just like she did with her ball. The bird spread his wings and rose from the water. Then, shoving his wings forward, he brought them down on top of the little pup.

Jeff raced into the water. He wasn't even as deep as his knees when he froze in his tracks. Even beneath his clothes, I could sense his whole body tighten—stiff as a board.

Mocha appeared on the surface behind the big bird. Water spewed from her nose as she snorted for breath. My tail wagged. She got away! Now Jeff wouldn't have to freeze to death, and maybe drown, trying to swim after her.

"Hurry, Mocha," I barked. "You're free. Swim for the bank."

Then my heart sank. The stupid mutt paddled around in a tight circle and went right back after the goose. Once more the wings spread wide. Snakelike head with beady, hateful eyes glared at the pup. He lurched, swooping on top of her—again!

Chapter 14

Although the water was only up to Jeff's waist, he was still shivering and barely able to move. When I swam past him, he yelled at me and grabbed, but he missed. I ignored him and just kept paddling.

Mocha fought her way to the surface a second time. She'd barely sucked in a breath when the giant bird lunged again and forced her back underneath the water.

My teeth ground together inside my head. Kicking with all fours—harder and faster than I even did when I chased quail—I raced for her.

The nasty old goose never saw me coming. The mean thing was concentrating so hard on holding Mocha under the water

with his wings, I was almost on top of him before he even noticed.

Snarling, I lunged. Sharp, angry teeth snapped shut.

He jerked forward and let out a loud squawk. I spit and gagged, trying to get rid of all the feathers that came out when he yanked. I didn't like the way they stuck to the roof of my mouth, but there was no time to worry about them now. As soon as he turned to attack me, I was ready. I'd grab him by the neck.

We'll see how *you* like having *your* head held under the water, I thought.

Only he didn't turn.

I heard a loud *HONK*. His wings spread and began to flap. Fast as a quail running through short grass, he knifed across the water, away from me. Wings flapping and big flat feet slapping the water, the goose flew back into the bright blue sky.

There was a little splash when Mocha bobbed back to the surface. She gagged and sputtered. Water poured in rivulets from her nose.

"You're safe," I told her. "Come on."

"Where'd he go? Where'd he go?" She swam in circles and looked all around with those wild brown eyes. "I almost had him. I've got to take him back to Jeff and Mandy. Where'd he go?"

"He flew away. Now, come on."

"What . . . what happened?" she gasped, water still dripping from her nose.

"You got goosed."

"What?" She frowned.

"You got goosed. You know—attacked by a goose. Now let's get out of here."

"But . . . but, I've got to bring him back, like I'm supposed to. Where'd he go? Where'd he go?"

My eyes rolled. Without another word, I leaned forward and nipped her right on the butt.

"Follow me! *NOW!*"

Her ears flattened. "Okay," she coughed.

When we swam past Jeff, he swooped Mocha up in his arms. I guess he was really cold, because he almost beat me back to the bank. My fur kept me warm, but I still didn't like the water. I shook and tried to get as much of it off as I could.

Usually, when I shook after a bath, Jeff yelled at me and ran away. This time when water droplets flew in all directions, he didn't seem to mind.

Mandy rushed to me, dropped to her knees, and gave me a great big hug.

"You're such a wonderful dog, T.P.," she cooed. "You saved the puppy. You're so brave. You're the most wonderful dog in the whole wide . . ."

I didn't hear the rest of what she said. I wiggled loose, raced down the bank, past the fallen tree, across the dam, and up the hill.

"I'll teach you to laugh at me," I roared. "I'll drag your scraggly behinds down to the pond and do the same thing I did to that goose. I'll . . ."

Eyes wide, the coyotes sprang from their hiding place in the briars. Tails tucked, they ran—didn't even take time to look back and see if I was still following.

Jeff whistled.

"T.P., come on. Quit chasing the coyotes. Let's go home."

Running as fast as they could, the three coyotes disappeared over the far hill. Tail straight up on one end and head high on the other, I kicked some grass at them and trotted back to Jeff.

THUNK!

I glanced up. Cord's crossed eyes kind of rolled around in his head. He staggered back from the chair leg he'd just bumped into and blinked a couple of times.

"Okay, dog," he said, finally focusing on me with one eye. "What's the deal?"

"What do you mean?" I shrugged an ear.

"Why all the fuss? Why is Jeff feeding you barbecue from his plate, instead of making you wait for scraps? And why does everybody keep petting you and telling you what a brave dog you are?"

I shrugged both ears this time. "Ah, it's no big deal. You know how Mocha is about chasing her ball."

Cord flipped his tail. "Yeah, I've seen them throw it in the pool and watched her chase it. Why? What happened?"

"Well, Mocha got goosed."

"Got what?"

"Goosed. You know—attacked by a goose."

"Oh, yeah." Cord's eyes crossed even more than usual. "Those big mean birds who live near the water."

I nodded. "Right. Anyway this goose landed in the pond and Mocha went after it, just like she does her ball. Only trouble, the thing was too big for her. It almost drowned her. So I had to . . . well . . . sort of help."

"I thought you didn't like water."

"I don't," I admitted. "But she's just a dumb little pup. The goose had a nest. Mocha wasn't bothering their eggs, though. There was no reason for that bird to try and hurt her. Then Jeff started after her. Only the water was so cold, he could hardly move. So . . . well . . . I had to do something."

Cord arched an eyebrow. "Were you scared?"

"I guess." I sighed. "But I didn't get scared or even think about it until *afterward*. You know, when I was walking home.

At the time, I was so mad at that bully bird for trying to hurt our puppy and so scared that Jeff was going to get hurt trying to save her . . . well . . . I just didn't have time to think."

Cord's whiskers arched on both ends of his smile.

"*Our* puppy?"

"Huh?" I frowned.

Cord's whiskers arched higher. "You said you didn't like that bully bird trying to hurt *our* puppy."

"I did? I said that?"

Jeff slipped me another piece of barbecued beef. That sauce was absolutely delicious.

"If she's gonna stay here," I said, licking my lips, "I guess she's *our* puppy. Guess we're going to have to help train her. As wild as she is, I know raising a puppy won't be easy, but . . ."

Wrapped in a couple of towels, Mocha was curled up on Mandy's lap—sound asleep.

". . . but she does have a sweet nature. Especially when she's asleep."

Cord flipped his tail. "Yeah. I guess you're right."

A brown eye peeked from beneath the towels in Mandy's lap. Suddenly a head popped up. In the blink of an eye, Mocha shook from the towels and landed just inches from Cord's tail. Cord took off like a shot.

With Mocha hot on his heels, he ricocheted off one chair leg, then another. Once in the open, he sprinted for the play-room. Both of them spun their feet on the linoleum.

In the other room, I heard the piano clang. Then there was a *thunk,* followed by an F-sharp (Cord must have landed on his bottom), then a *BLAM* when he finally hit the floor.

Wagging her tail like she'd just done something really special, Mocha trotted back. She leaned over and stuck her nose right in my face.

"You see that? The cat ran from me. That was fun.

"Do you like to chase the cat?

"Why do they call him a cat?

"Why did you save me from the goose? Was it because you like me?

"Huh? Huh? I like you. Do you like me?"

"*GEERRRRR!*"

"T.P.," Jeff called from above me. "Be nice to the puppy."

She licked and kissed me all over the face. I glared at her with my meanest look—but on my other end, I could hear my tail thumping. It bounced between two of the chair legs, beating away like a drum.

Like I said—raising a puppy won't be easy.